Koch

THE CANTERVILLE GHOST

GRAFISK FORLAG *Copenhagen*

GYLDENDAL NORSK FORLAG *Oslo*

EMC CORP. *St. Paul, Minnesota, U.S.A.*

ERNST KLETT VERLAG *Stuttgart*

ESSELTE STUDIUM *Stockholm*

EDIZIONI SCOLASTICHE MONDADORI *Milan*

BORDAS EDITEUR *Paris*

JOHN MURRAY *London*

TAMMI *Helsinki*

ASAHI SHUPPANSHA *Tokyo*

WOLTERS/NOORDHOFF *Groningen*

EDICIONES TORAY *Barcelona*

GRAFICA EDITÔRA PRIMOR *Rio de Janeiro*

OSCAR WILDE

THE CANTERVILLE GHOST

EASY READERS
ER
EASY READERS

The vocabulary is based on
Salling/Hvid: English-Danish Basic Dictionary
Weis: Grund- und Aufbauwortschatz, Englisch
Thorndike: The Teacher's Word Book
West: A General Service List

EDITORS

Aage Salling
Erik Hvid *Denmark*

ADVISERS

Marja Wuorenheimo *Finland*
Otto Weise *Germany*
G. de Groot *The Netherlands*
Erling Rundstrøm *Norway*
Torkel Nöjd *Sweden*

Cover design: Ib Jørgensen
Illustrations: Oskar Jørgensen

ISBN Denmark 87 429 7440 2

Printed in Denmark by
Grafisk Institut A·S Copenhagen
MCMLXXIV

I

When Mr. Hiram B. Otis, the American Minister, bought Canterville Chase, everyone told him that it was not a very wise thing to do because it was well-known that there was a ghost in the place. Lord Canterville had felt that he must tell Mr. Otis about it when he came to talk about the *price.*

"I must tell you, Mr. Otis," he said, "that many living people have seen the ghost, and that we do not want to live at Canterville Chase any longer. He almost *scared* the life out of my sister by putting his hands on her

---

price: the sum of money you must pay for a thing if you want to buy it.

scare: make very much afraid, put fear into.

arms while she was dressing. After that none of our younger *servants* would stay with us in the castle, and Lady Canterville often got very little sleep at night because of the sounds that came from the *corridor* and some of the rooms."

"My Lord," answered Mr. Otis, "I come from a modern country where we don't believe in ghosts. I'll take the castle at the price you want."

"I am almost sure that the ghost is there," said Lord Canterville. "It has been well-known for three hundred years, and it is always seen before the death of people who live in the castle."

"So is the family doctor, Lord Canterville, but there is no such thing as a ghost."

"If you don't mind a ghost in the house it is all right, but now I have told you about it."

A few weeks after this Mr. Otis and his family went down to Canterville Chase. There were Mr. Otis himself, his wife, a beautiful

servant

corridor: long room into which many doors open.

New York lady, Washington, their eldest son, Virginia, a little girl of fifteen, and two boys who were *twins*.

Canterville Chase is seven miles from the nearest railway station, and Mr. Otis had telegraphed for a carriage to meet them. It was a fine July evening, and the sky was blue. But as they drove up to the castle a swarm of big black birds flew over their heads, the sky became dark, and some big drops of rain began to fall.

---

twins: two children born at the same time from the same mother.

"I welcome you to Canterville Chase," said an old woman who was standing on the steps to receive them. This was Mrs. Umney, the *housekeeper.* They followed her into the house and came into a long, low room with a large window. Here they sat down and looked round while Mrs. Umney served the tea.

"Something has been spilt here," said Mrs. Otis and pointed to a large red *stain* on the floor.

"Yes," said Mrs. Umney, "it is blood."

"I don't like that," Mrs. Otis went on. "It must be taken away at once."

"It is the blood of Lady Eleanore Canterville, who was killed on that very place by her own husband, Sir Simon Canterville, in 1575. He lived here nine years after her death; and then he was never seen *alive* again. But

---

housekeeper: head servant.
alive: not dead.

his ghost still walks about the castle. The blood-stain cannot be taken away."

"Yes, it can," said Mr. Otis. "I have got something here that will take it away," and before the old woman could do anything to stop him, he took out a small black stick and *rubbed* the stain with it. "Now it is gone," he said. "I knew I could do it."

But as soon as he had said these words a *flash of lightning* filled the room with a

strong light, and a *peal of thunder* rolled through the house. They all sprang to their

---

rubbed: moved his stick up and down on the stain to take it away.

peal of thunder: a strong sound that follows the flash of lightning.

feet. "I have seen things with my own eyes," said Mrs. Umney, "that would make your hair stand on end, and many a night I have not closed an eye for the *awful* things that are done here."

Mr. and Mrs. Otis, however, told the old woman that they were not afraid of ghosts, and then she left the family to go to her own room.

Questions

1. What is Canterville Chase?
2. Why was Mr. Otis not afraid of ghosts?
3. When did black birds fly over the castle?
4. Where had the stain of blood come from?
5. What did they hear when Mr. Otis had taken away the stain of blood?

---

awful things: things that scared her, made her afraid.

2

There was lightning and thunder all that night. The next morning when they came down to *breakfast*, they found the *terrible* stain of blood on the floor again. "I have tried to rub it away," said Washington. "It must be the ghost." He rubbed out the stain again, but the second morning it was there again. And the third morning also it was there, though Mr. Otis had locked the door to the room himself and taken the *key* with him upstairs. The whole family were interested now.

---

breakfast: you eat breakfast in the morning.
terrible: awful.

The day had been nice and warm, and in the evening the family went out for a drive in the carriage. They did not come home till nine o'clock, when they had *supper*. At eleven o'clock they went to bed, and by half past eleven all the lights were out. Some time after, Mr. Otis heard *a strange noise* in the corridor outside his room. He got up and looked at his *watch*. It was one o'clock. The noise did not stop, and now he heard footsteps. He opened the door, and there he saw a terrible old man. Long white hair fell down from his head, his eyes were like fire, and heavy chains were hanging from his hands and ankles.

"My dear sir," said Mr. Otis, "you must not make such a noise. Here is some oil for your

---

supper: you eat supper in the evening.
a strange noise: a strong sound he had not heard before.
watch: on your watch you can see what time it is.

chains. I shall leave it here in the corridor and I shall give you more later on." And with these words Mr. Otis closed his door and went to bed again.

For a short time the Canterville ghost stood quite still. Then he threw the bottle on the floor and ran down the corridor, while he sent out a terrible green light. Just when he came to the end of the corridor, a door was *quietly* opened and someone threw a large pillow at his head. He would have to get away – so he went through the wall. And the house became *quiet* again.

---

quiet, quietly: there was no noise.

When he came to his small room in the left *wing* of the castle, he sat down to think. Never before had anybody done such things to him.

He thought of Lord Canterville's sister, whom he had almost scared the life out of; of the four girls who had run away and never come back only because he had *grinned* at them through the window; of the old woman who had seen him sitting in her chair one morning and had been ill in bed for a long time. He thought of the servant who had shot himself with a revolver because he had seen a green hand on the window – all these great things came back to him, and now these Americans gave him oil for his chains and threw

---

grin: smile so that the teeth can be seen.

pillows at his face. He certainly would have to do something and he spent the whole night thinking of what he could do.

Questions

1. Who tried to take away the stain of blood?
2. What did Mr. Otis hear in the corridor?
3. What did Mr. Otis ask the ghost to do?
4. Why did the ghost think that he would have to do something?

3

The next morning when the Otis family met at breakfast, they talked about the ghost. "I am very sorry he did not want to have the oil for his chains," said Mr. Otis, "but if he does not use it, we must take his chains from him. And it is not at all nice of you to throw pillows at his head," Mr. Otis went on, speaking to the twins, who began to laugh.

For the rest of the week they saw nothing of the ghost. The only thing was that the stain of blood came out again every morning, but never in the same colour. The only person who did not laugh when they talked about the ghost, was little Virginia, who became very *sad* when she saw the blood-stain, and nearly *cried* one morning when it was quite green.

One Sunday night just after they had gone to bed, they heard a terrible noise in the hall. They ran downstairs and saw that a large suit of armour had fallen on the stone floor, and

---

sad: very sorry.

cried: she cried because she was so sad.

sitting in a high chair was the Canterville ghost. Mr. Otis took out his revolver and told the ghost to hold up his hands. The ghost got up with a *cry* and ran past them, putting out the light and leaving them in the dark hall. At the top of the steps he stopped and gave a terrible laugh. It rolled through the hall, echoed, and died away. A door opened, and Mrs. Otis came out. "I am afraid you are not well," she said, "and I have brought you a bottle of medicine which will be very good for you."

---

cry: he gave a cry because he got afraid.

The ghost looked at her, very angry, and then began to turn himself into a big, black dog. But the sound of footsteps made him change his mind, and when the twins came up to him, they found him only as a spot of green light moving out through the wall.

In his room he sat down, very sad. He had hoped that a ghost in armour would have scared the family. It was his own suit of armour, and Queen Elizabeth herself had said that she liked it very much. But when he had put it on, it was much too heavy for him, and he had fallen on the floor and hurt his leg.

For some days he was very ill, and only left his room to keep the stain of blood in order. He would, however, try once more to scare the family, and he would do it on Friday the 17th of August. In the evening it began to rain, and the wind was so strong that all the doors and windows *shook*. He liked that.

His plan was this: First he would go to Washington's room, make terrible sounds from the foot of the boy's bed and put a knife three times through his own head to the sound of *slow* music. Next he would go into the room of the American minister and his wife, put a cold hand on Mrs. Otis's head and say terrible things into Mr. Otis's ear. He did not know what to do to little Virginia; she was a nice girl, and had never done anything to him. But then there were the twins. The first thing he would do, of course, was to sit on them, which

shook: moved up and down and from side to side.
slow: not fast.

would give them *nightmares*; then he would go down on all fours, and crawl round their bed, looking at them with one big, green eye and laugh until they were deadly scared.

At half past ten he heard the family going to bed. He could hear the twins laughing and making a noise, but at a quarter past eleven all was still. He stepped out of the wall with a bad smile on his mouth, and walked down the corridor to Washington's door. He laughed to himself and turned the corner – and then he fell back against the wall and hid his white face in his long hands. In front of him was a terrible ghost. It had no hair; its face was round, and fat, and white; there was a

---

nightmare: terrible dream.

terrible grin on its mouth, and fire came out of it. From the eyes came a strong red light, and in its right hand was a big sword. The Canterville ghost was very much afraid. He had never seen a ghost before, so he turned round and ran back to his room as fast as he could.

All night he lay on his bed, white and scared, until just before the morning came, when he made his way to the place where he had seen the other ghost. After all two ghosts were better than one, and he might make a friend who could help him with the twins.

But *a fearful sight* met him. The other ghost was leaning against the wall; the light had

---

a fearful sight: what he saw filled him with fear.

gone out of its eyes, the sword had fallen from its hand, and when the Canterville ghost took him by the arm, he fell to the floor. And there was the Canterville ghost holding in his arms a *pillow*, a *broom*, a *turnip* and a large piece of paper with some words written on it.

They had played a trick on him. The old Canterville look came into his eyes, he raised his hand towards the door of the room of the twins as if to say that he would come back, and moved away to his room.

Questions

1. Who did not laugh when they spoke about the ghost?

2. What did they see on the floor of the hall?

3. What did Mrs. Otis say to the ghost?

4. Why did the ghost run away as fast as he could when he saw the other ghost?

5. Who had put up the broom and the turnip to make them look like a ghost?

4

For five days he did not go out of his room, and at last gave up keeping the blood-stain in order. If the Otis family did not want it, he was not going to look after it any more. He had to walk in the corridor one night every week, and to make his terrible sounds from the large window in the east on the first and third Wednesday in every month. It is true that his life had not been good at all, but nobody could say that he did not do his job as a ghost well.

For the next three Saturdays he walked down the corridor between 12 o'clock and 3 o'clock in the night, but he did his best not to make any noise. He took off his boots and

oiled his chains – he had taken the bottle from Mr. Otis's bedroom while the family were having supper.

Still the twins did not leave him alone. They put up *strings* across the corridor and put out oil on the floor, and one night he fell and hurt his right arm. This made him very

angry, so he thought that he would go to the boys' room the next night as "The *Headless* Man".

At eleven o'clock he began to take out his things. When he had dressed, he put on his large boots, found his pistols, and at last at a quarter past one he came out of the wall and walked down the corridor. When he got to the room where the twins slept, he found the door half open. He stopped – then he opened it and went in. There was a noise and

---

headless: with no head.

a heavy *bucket* of water fell down, making him wet to the skin, and it nearly fell on his right arm. At the same time he heard a laugh from the big bed. He got a shock and ran back to his room as fast as he could, and the next day he had a temperature and had to stay in bed. The only good thing was that he had not taken his head with him, for had he done so, what might not have happened?

He now gave up all hope of scaring the family, and took great care not to make any noise when he walked up and down in the house. But the twins did not leave him alone, and one night when he had gone down to look at the family portraits in the hall and to see if

there was anything left of the blood-stain, the two boys sprang upon him and cried "BOO!!" in his ear. He ran up the steps to the corridor, only to meet Washington, who was waiting for him with a big garden-*syringe*. The only way for him to get away was through the wall.

After this the family did not see him again, and everybody thought that he had gone away. Mrs. Otis gave a big *party*, which everybody in the district talked about, Mr. Otis began to write a book, the twins played

---

party: if you ask many people to tea or dinner, we can say that you have a party.

in the garden, and Virginia rode about the fields on her little horse together with one of her friends, a young man, who had come to Canterville for the last week of his *holidays*.

Questions

1. Where had the ghost taken the bottle of oil?

2. Why did he fall in the corridor?

3. Why did he want to go to the boys' room as "The Headless Man"?

4. What did Washington use the syringe for?

---

holiday: time when you do not work.

5

One day when Virginia and her friend came back from a ride on their horses, she went up by a back door. She did not want anybody to see her. As she was running down the corridor, she thought that she saw someone in a bedroom. The door was open, and she looked in to see who it was. And there was the Canterville ghost himself! He was sitting

by the window, looking at the trees in the garden outside. Virginia's first idea was to run away, but he looked so sad that she felt sorry for him and thought that she would go in and speak to him. She walked in – so quietly that he did not hear her until she spoke to him.

"I am sorry for you," she said, "but my brothers are going away tomorrow, and then, if you are a good ghost, we shall all leave you alone."

"Do not ask me to be good. I must walk about at night, if that is what you mean," answered the ghost. "That is why I am here."

"No, that is not true," she said, "you have been very bad; Mrs. Umney told us the first day we were here that you killed your wife."

"Well, that is true," said the ghost, "but it was a family *matter*, and only the family should care about it. No other persons had anything to do with it."

"It is very wrong to kill anyone," said Virginia.

"My wife was not very beautiful, she did not care about my dress, and she was a very bad cook. But it is all over now, and I don't

---

matter: question, problem; a family matter: a thing that only the family could talk to him about.

think it was very nice of her brothers to let me die of *hunger* even if I killed her."

"Oh, Mr. Ghost – I mean Sir Simon, are you *hungry*? Would you like to have something to eat?"

"No, thank you, I never eat anything now, but it is very good of you; you are much nicer than the rest of your terrible family."

"Stop!" cried Virginia, stamping her foot. "It is you who are terrible. You know you

---

hunger: he died because they gave him nothing to eat.

hungry: you are hungry if you have had nothing to eat for a long time.

took the colours out of my box to keep that blood-stain in order. You took all my reds and yellows and greens, yes, all my colours. I shall go to *papa* and ask him to keep the twins at home for another week!"

"Please, don't go, Miss Virginia," he cried. "I am so unhappy; I don't know what to do. I want to go to sleep and I cannot."

"Of course you can. You just go to bed and put out the light," said Virginia.

"I have not slept for three hundred years,"

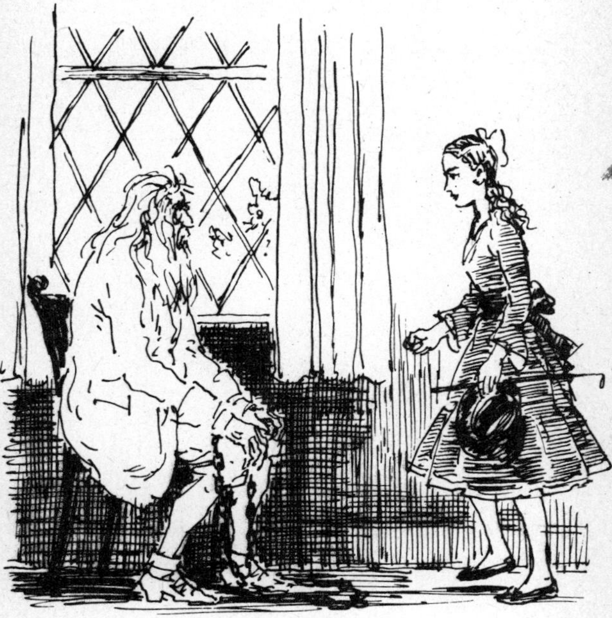

---

papa: father.

he said sadly. "For three hundred years I have not slept, and I am *tired*."

Virginia came up to him and looked into his old face. "Poor, poor ghost," she said, "have you no place where you can sleep?"

"There is a garden behind the woods. There the grass grows long and the birds sing all night; all night they sing; it would be good to sleep there."

"You mean the Garden of Death?" she said.

"Yes, Death. Death must be beautiful. To lie in the *soft*, brown earth with the grass growing over one's head – and the *silence*! To have no yesterday and no tomorrow, to *forget* time, to forget life. You can help me. You can open Death's door to me, for Love is always with you, and Love is stronger than Death."

Virginia turned white in the face, and she shook all over. She felt as if she was in a terrible dream.

The ghost spoke again: "Have you ever read the verse on the window of the room in which the blood-stain is?"

---

tired: if you work hard for a long time you will be tired.

soft: not hard.

silence: there are no sounds at all, and nobody talking.

forget: not remember; not think of.

"Oh, often!" cried the little girl, looking up; "I know it quite well. There are only six lines:

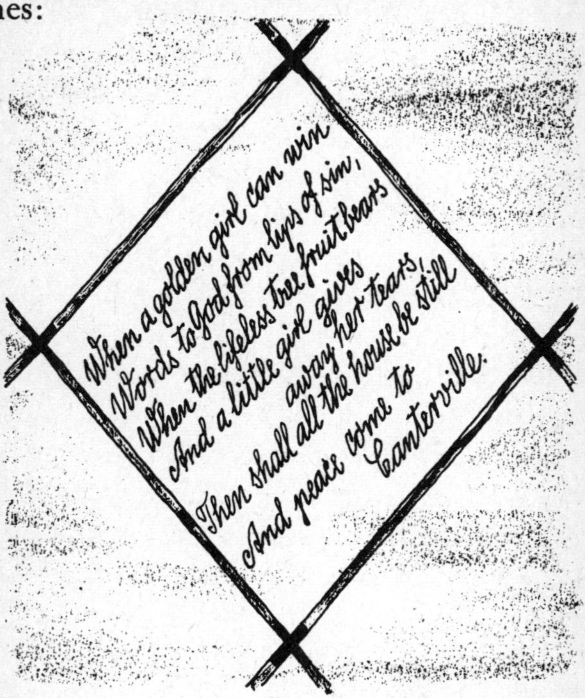

---

golden: with yellow hair of the same colour as gold.

lips: the lips form the opening of the mouth.

sin: bad thing you have done; his sin was that he had killed his wife. – It means that a girl with golden hair could make him talk to God.

lifeless: dead.

fruit: an apple is a fruit; *fruit bears:* has fruit.

tears: when you cry, tears come to your eyes.

peace: no ghost would walk about the castle any more, making a noise and scaring people.

"But I don't know what they mean," Virginia said.

"They mean," said the ghost, "that you must *weep* for me because I have no tears, and help me to *pray* to God because I don't believe in God, and then, if you have been good, Death will be good to me. You will see terrible things, but they will not *harm* you, for your love is too great for them."

The ghost looked down at Virginia's golden head. After some time she stood up. "I will come," she said. "I am not afraid."

He got up and took her hand and kissed it. His fingers were as cold as ice, and his lips burned like fire, but Virginia was not afraid as he walked with her through the dark room. She felt that the pictures on the walls looked at her, and she heard them cry, "Go back,

---

weep: cry.
pray: help him to ask God to let him die.
harm: they would not do anything bad to her.

little girl! Go back!" But Virginia did not go back. When they got to the other end of the room, the ghost stopped and said some words she could not hear, and then she saw the wall open. A cold wind came out. "Quick, quick," cried the ghost, "or it will be too late," and *in a moment* the wall had closed behind them, and the bedroom was *empty.*

Questions

1. Why did Virginia go in by the back door?

2. Who was in the room?

3. Why had Sir Simon killed his wife?

4. Why did Virginia ask the ghost if he would have something to eat?

5. Why would death be a beautiful thing for the ghost?

6. Why could the bad things not harm Virginia?

---

in a moment: very soon, quickly.
empty: there was no one in the room.

About ten minutes later the Otis family came down to have tea, and as Virginia did not come down, Mrs. Otis sent the twins up to find her. Virginia often went out to pick flowers for the table, so Mrs. Otis *was not worried* about her.

But when it was 6 o'clock, and she had not come back, she sent the boys out to find her, while she herself and Mr. Otis looked in every room in the house. They were all very much afraid now. Mr. Otis sent a telegram to the

was not worried: thought that nothing was wrong.

police and asked them to look out for little Virginia, and then he asked the family to sit down to supper, told a servant to bring round his horse, and rode down the Ascot Road. He had gone about a mile when he heard a horse behind him, and when he looked round he saw Virginia's friend coming up at a gallop.

"I'm very sorry, Mr. Otis," he said, "but I can't eat any supper as long as Virginia is not found. You won't send me back, will you? I can't go! I won't go!"

"Well, Cecil, if you won't go back then you must come along with me."

They galloped on to the railway station, but nobody there had seen Virginia. At eleven o'clock they came back, very tired and very sad. They found Washington and the twins waiting for them on the road. They, too, had been out looking for Virginia, but they had not found her.

When they had got into the castle, Mr. Otis told them all to go to bed, saying that they could do nothing more that night.

Just as they were coming out of the sitting-room they heard the clock strike twelve. A terrible peal of thunder shook the whole house, part of the wall at the top of the steps opened with a loud noise, and Virginia came out very white in the face with a small box in her hand. In a moment they had run up to her, and Mrs. Otis, with tears in her eyes, took her in her arms.

"Where have you been, child?" asked Mr. Otis. "We have been all over the district to find you."

"Thank God you have been found," said Mrs. Otis. "But you must never leave us in that way again."

"Papa, I have been with the ghost. He is dead, and you must come and see him. He had been a very bad man, but he was sorry for all that he had done, and he gave me this beautiful box before he died."

The whole family just looked at her – they could not say anything. After some time Virginia turned round and walked through the opening in the wall and down a corridor, and the rest of the family followed her. At the end of the corridor there was a heavy door, and when Virginia put her hand on it, it opened, and they found themselves in a little room with one small window. In the wall there was a heavy ring with chains hanging down from it, and in the chains a *skeleton.* Virginia put her little hands together and looked at it, and the others looked at it too, very surprised.

"Hallo!" cried one of the twins, who had stood looking out of the window to find out which wing of the castle they were in. "The old tree under the sitting-room window is green again. And I can see that there are apples on it."

Skeleton

"God *has forgiven him*," said Virginia. As she spoke the others looked at her, and it seemed to them that her face was shining with a beautiful light.

Questions

1. Why was Mrs. Otis not worried about Virginia at first?
2. Where did Mr. Otis and Cecil go to find Virginia?
3. What did they hear when they saw Virginia?
4. What did Virginia show them?

---

has forgiven him: is no longer angry with him.

Four days later they took Sir Simon to the Garden of Death. At eleven o'clock at night four carriages started from Canterville Chase. Lord Canterville was there, Mr. and Mrs. Otis, Washington and the twins, and Virginia. And in the last carriage was Mrs. Umney.

They placed him in a deep grave in a corner of the Garden under an old tree. Virginia covered his grave with flowers. As she did so the moon came out, and the birds began to sing. When she thought of what the ghost had said about the Garden of Death,

her eyes filled with tears, and she could not say a word on her way back to the castle.

The next morning, before Lord Canterville went up to town, Mr. Otis spoke with him.

"My lord," he said, "here are some *jewels* which were in the box that Sir Simon gave Virginia. It is quite clear to me that these jewels should be in your family, and Virginia is too young for them. But she would be very happy if you would be so kind as to let her have the box they were in."

"My dear sir," answered Lord Canterville, "your daughter was very kind to Sir Simon, and my family is very thankful to her for what she did for him. The jewels are hers. I think that if I took them from her, the old man would be out of his grave again in two weeks. The castle is yours, and everything that is in it."

Mr. Otis was sorry that Lord Canterville would not take the jewels, and asked him to think it over again. But the answer was no. – And on the day when Virginia *was married* to young Cecil she wore the jewels, and everybody thought how beautiful they were.

In the afternoon of that happy day Virginia and Cecil walked down to the Garden of Death to look at Sir Simon's grave. "Virginia," said Cecil, "there is something you should tell me."

"What is that, Cecil dear?"

"You have never told me what happened to you when you were in that room alone with the ghost."

"I have never told anyone," she said.

"I know, but you might tell me."

"Don't ask me, Cecil. I cannot tell you. Poor Sir Simon! He made me see what Life is, and what Death is, and why Love is stronger than both."

"You need not tell me as long as I have your *heart*."

---

was married: became Cecil's wife.

heart: as long as I have your heart: as long as you love me.

"You have always had that, Cecil."

"And you will tell our children some day, won't you?"

Virginia turned red.

Questions

1. Who took Sir Simon to the Garden of Death?

2. What did Lord Canterville say would happen if he took the jewels?

3. Where did Virginia and Cecil go on the day they were married?

4. What had Virginia learnt from Sir Simon?